A Prelude For Murder

D E McCluskey
&
Tony Bolland

D E McCluskey & Tony Bolland

A Prelude for Murder

ISBN: 978-1-914381-39-3

Dammaged Productions

www.dammaged.com

For Wyndham
Serious devotion to a cause that seemed hopeless…
Quite a few times

1.

I HATE AUDITION day. It always brings all the failings in my life back into my consciousness. Failings that are not necessarily my fault. I mean, It wasn't my fault my father's genes, mingling with my mother's, would produce a boy of a little less than average height, a boy with thinner hair than most of the other boys, and who was susceptible to the polio virus.

It found me and hit hard when I was six years of age. My mother would tell me she thought I was going to *go the way of Peter*. Apparently, Peter was an older brother of mine, who didn't make it past the age of three. I never did get to find out what *the way of Peter* was, but apparently it was not a good thing.

It seemed God had other ideas for me, or so my mother used to tell me when it became apparent, I would survive the polio. 'George, you must have a purpose in life,' she would say. 'The good Lord has spared you. You're part of his plans.'

To this day I still haven't been able to figure out what that purpose could be. Maybe one day it will become clear, but until then, I think I'll ride this particular train solo. I don't need anyone else to steer my ship, but me.

My father had a plan for me, although my mother would never approve of it.

I survived polio relatively unscathed. That is if you can call a stunted leg, coupled with a club foot unscathed. I suppose I was lucky. A lot of other children, and I mean a lot, were nowhere near as lucky as me.

'Praise the Sweet Baby Jesus,' My mother would command me, forcing me to kneel at the side of the bed, in prayer, before bedtime. 'You need to thank him for every single day, George. You're a living miracle.'

Sometimes, when I'd done something wrong, or if I'd been lazy, or if I'd talked back, she'd shout at me. 'The Lord Jesus didn't spare you to disrespect your mother and father. Why would you want to laugh in the face of your gift and shame us?'

She never, ever let up on the ingrained Catholic guilt, which is why I probably gravitated towards my father's company, rather than hers. In my eyes, he had the right idea. He didn't go for the readings and followings of the prophet Jesus Christ but chose to immerse himself into the deep religion of music.

He was a drummer in a touring band. This took him away more often than not, so when he *was* home it was always a very special time for me.

I knew he loved my mother. When I look back on their relationship, I can see he had a deep love and respect for her, but I can also see that he couldn't live within the confines, within the cloud, or thick mist, of her religion.

'It's the devil's own music he play's, George. It is. He used to be such a good, Godfearing man, but now... now he's changed. You stay here with your mother, and your faith. Don't be listening to the stories of his drunken debauchery and ungodly practices. You stay here, with me, and I'll keep you safe. I'll keep you clothed and fed.' She would pull the young and impressionable George Hogg to her ample bosom and almost smother him in love.

2.

MY FATHER WAS one of the lucky ones. He'd come home from the Great War. A huge number of my friend's fathers didn't. My mother used to tell me she didn't think he'd come home either. This would confuse me, especially when he was sitting there, in our back room, a glass of milk stout in his hand and his flat cap pitched to one side. I remember asking once what she meant. She looked at me with as stern a look as she had ever given anyone in her life. A sneer formed on her face, and her eyes narrowed.

'The Devil took that one, on the fields of Flanders. His heart is as back as the centre of a poppy.'

Once again, I had no idea what she was talking about.

'You'll understand when you're older,' was the only explanation she would ever give.

Growing up, I was never what you would call a popular kid on the streets of Liverpool. Maybe it was because my mother would never allow me to have friends over without them sitting through at least half an hour of prayers before going upstairs to play pirates. Or maybe it was because I was shorter than all the other boys, underweight, and had a metal calliper strapped to my leg.

On hindsight, it was probably the latter, but I never let it get to me, too much. I never had much interest in football, or even cricket, so most of my friends tended to be girls.

I was always the *husband* when we played house, or the doctor in the hospital, or the vet when a poor teddy bear was ill. To be honest, it didn't bother me much. Yes, I was teased, quite a bit by the other boys, but that was all forgotten about when my father came home.

When he was home, I was a king.

My father was a hero in Bootle.

Not only was he a war veteran, but he was a jazz musician too.

Bootle is mostly a dirty old dock town nestling on the River Mersey, on the outskirts of the bustling port of Liverpool. It would be realistic to say that roughly seventy percent of the men folk worked either on the dock itself, or from a fringe industry that related to them. The town was poor, yes, but it was rich in personality, culture, and diversity.

My father was part of all three.

He worked away a lot of the time, playing drums for big bands the length and breadth of the country. A few times a year he might even travel further afield, into Europe, and I'm sure that once or twice he boasted of playing the White Star Liner ships, travelling all the way to America.

When he was home, my mother would soften. That's how I know she loved him. For all the other times she'd curse his name and cross herself whenever he was mentioned, she took him back, every single time. There would be parties in our house, and for a short time it would be a loving, exciting, vibrant place to be.

I would, all of a sudden, become the most popular boy on the street. Everyone wanted to be my friend, and of course I'd allow them to be... for a small price.

I learned the art of making the best out of a situation, from a young age.

In order to come to one of my father's parties, or more likely, sneak into one of my father's parties, you had to pay. It was nothing too expensive, nothing too much, sometimes it would just be a favour, other times it might be food, but there was always a payment to be made.

3.

WHEN I WAS eleven, my father hadn't been home for almost a year. My mother was spending all the time she had not working in the dairy, worshipping in church. Her religious fever had gone into overdrive.

The polio I had suffered had stunted more than just the growth in my leg, it had stunted my physical growth too. I was much smaller than the other boys. Where they were all growing broad chests and the forerunner of facial hair, I was still small and almost cherub like in my appearance. The boys were starting to talk in deeper tones, but I was still young and squeaky. This was when my mother forced me to join the church choir.

Well, she never actually forced me, but she lay damn near enough Irish Catholic guilt on my shoulders that it felt very much like force.

Tears would flow every time I told her I didn't want to go. 'The good Lord gave you that voice George, he gave it to you to rejoice in him,' she would say. 'All the Hogg men have let me down. You won't sing for me, your no-mark father is nowhere to be found, and even your older brother Peter didn't stay around...'

I always thought the Peter remark was a tad below the belt, even for a die-in-the-wool catholic, trying her best to get her only son back on the path of righteousness. But I fell for it every time, hook line and sinker, and off to choir practice I'd go.

Once again, I was the only boy, well the only boy of remotely my own age. All the others were well under ten and going all guns blazing in the falsetto for Jesus' campaign.

The one thing I did get from my four years of choir practice was the opportunity to stretch my vocal talents, and I rapidly went from being able to carry a tune, to being able to hold a tune, in at least four different octaves.

When I was twelve, very near my thirteenth birthday, two major things happened in my life. One was the result of another.

My mother, the pillar of virtue and Godliness that she was, disappeared out of my life completely.

One day she was there, licking her hand and rubbing down a rogue piece of hair on the top of my head on my way to school, and the next she was gone. All that was left of her was a note on the table when I got home from school.

I never kept the letter, I didn't think it was important to keep it at the time, but it went something like this:

My dearest George,

You know I love you more than anything in the whole word, and I know that you are, deep down a good and faithful child. I have lived in the shadow of the Good Lord all of my life, while the demons of Satan have run amok around me. First, your father. He was the true love of my life, but the Great War took something from him, something was lost deep in his soul, and no matter how hard I tried to keep him in the light, he always wavered in the end.

Well, now it seems it is my turn to waver…

That's all I can really remember, but I know that it went on to say that basically, the Lord was giving a lot more than just his good word around the parish. Apparently, Fr Dawson was also sowing his seed. And some of that seed was sown in my mother's field.

She'd been having an affair with the priest for the last year, ever since my father had left the last time, and she was now pregnant. She and Fr Dawson had run away together, apparently they had gone to live in a little place called Jersey. It's a small island somewhere by France.

Auntie Joan from next door was going to look after me, until the Devil himself could find it in his dark heart to come home and take over his fatherly duties.

That was the second thing that happened.

My father came home, this time for good.

4.

MY FATHER CAME home, and this time for good.

It feels good saying that line, it makes me think that everything I'm going to relay to you will be nice, rosy, walk in the park…

He did come home, and this time, he told me, it was for good.

He came back and moved in. Auntie Joan from next door seemed pleased to see him. Her face would redden every time she looked at him, and I was old enough to notice that most of the women, of a certain age, usually did the same.

But Auntie Joan was also happy to see him because it meant she could relinquish her responsibility of me.

We didn't see eye to eye, me and good old Auntie Joan. She thought I was spying on her daughters when they were getting undressed for bed at night. Of course, I *was* spying on them, they were delightful creatures. They would tease me because of my height and my gimp leg, and some of them (there were four, all of them beautiful) would brush past and smile at me.

I was only small, but I was hormonal, and hormonal boys are going to do what hormonal boys do.

So, when my father came home, she brushed me off, back next door. 'Maybe George Senior will be able to knock that dirty devil out of you,' she remarked as I left the house for the last time.

'So, what's all this I hear about you trying to look up Millie's skirts?' He asked when we were finally alone in the house.

I was scared, I'd never been alone with the man in the whole of my thirteen years.

I hung my head low; my cheeks reddening at getting caught in the act.

He reached out to me over the small dining table and grabbed my chin, not roughly, but strong enough to command my attention.

'Listen to me laddie,' his accent was strange now, all the years of travelling I supposed. 'Listen to me. It's only normal that you'd want to see Millie's under crackers, Jesus, she a damn fine looking girl for her age.'

'But… but she's my cousin, isn't she? Her mum is Auntie Joan.'

George Senior laughed then. He laughed and smiled a lot, but that time I'll remember for the rest of my life, because the laugh was just for me. It wasn't a show for anyone else.

It was all mine.

'Oh, Christ no. Millie isn't your cousin son. We just call old Joan over there Auntie as she lives next door. Jesus Christ lad, you could bang the seven bells of Hades out of that girl, and there wouldn't be a hint of sin in it.'

I never knew what *the seven belles of Hades* were, but to an underweight twelve year old boy, they sounded good.

5.

MY FATHER AND I had a fantastic relationship. I had a look of him, everyone said it, but I was never able to see it. Where my father was tall and broad, I was small and narrow. Where his face was rugged and stubbled, mine was chubby and smooth. But our eyes, that was where the similarity was, we both had the deepest blue eyes.

He took me everywhere with him. Because I was still only a boy, and had to attend school for a few years yet, he could only take local gigs as a drummer, but there were many bands around the pubs and clubs of Liverpool in need of a serious drummer. The only problem was that he had a runty little thirteen year old in tow.

I soon got used to sleeping in dressing rooms, to the incessant pounding of American jazz, or moody blues. Some of the music I would hear him play was, how would my mother put it now? "The Devil's own music!"

I loved it, and I wanted to play it.

'Dad, how do you do that? How do you get them drums to sound like you do?' I asked him once on the way home to Bootle from a gig in the centre of Liverpool.

'Why don't I show you? Would you like that Georgie lad?'

I laughed as we walked down the cold wet Dock Road. 'I can't play like that, I've got this remember,' I said tapping my metal calliper as I spoke. 'I'll never be able to be like you.'

He stopped dead in the street, the rain was soaking us through. I continued to walk, but when I noticed he wasn't walking with me anymore, I turned to face him. I was more than a little scared of that look.

He was shaking his head as he looked at me. 'No Georgie, you don't want to be like me. You want to be you; however, you are. Don't you EVER try to fit in laddie. You allow others to want you in, and if they don't, then tell them fuck the hell off.'

I recoiled at the curse word. 'I'd heard a few of the older boys say it, mostly to each other, but I'd never heard a grown man say it to a child. The word stung a little.

'Dad?' I asked, still scared of the look on his face.

'No son. I won't apologise. I mean it, fuck them the hell off. You're a fantastic kid, you can be anything you want to be. That's why I came back, to show you how to be yourself.'

He knelt down in the middle of the cobbled road and called me over. 'Think hard on this laddie, think hard about what, and who, you want to be. I don't want you to be me son…' he was shaking his head again now, '…no, I want you to be the best of what you can be. So, tell me, and tell me true son. What do you want to be?'

The rain was pouring down my face now, and I was glad, because it hid the tears falling from my eyes and running down my cheeks.

'I want to play drums dad. I really do.'

He stood up then, he wrapped his arms around me and hugged me, tight. 'Then that's what you are going to do laddie, that what you're going to do.'

The rest of the walk was in silence, it wasn't an awkward silence, more of a contented one.

6.

THE VERY NEXT week he presented me with something that changed the course of my life. Maybe I'd like to say it changed it for the better, maybe it did, but it also exposed me to corruptions that eventually I found I had very little control of.

I was sat in the front room of the house, the weather had started to get warmer, and I remember marvelling at a shaft of light that was beaming in from the front window of the parlour. The dust mites playing in that shaft held my attention a lot more than the book I was attempting to read.

My father was home, but I hadn't seen much of him over the last few days, he'd been spending a lot of time in the foundry on Brasenose Road. He had friends who worked there, and he would hang around, drinking with them on the days when he wasn't working. But this week he'd spent more time with them than ever. Each night he'd come home with a mischievous twinkle in his eye, smiling and laughing. When he was in this kind of mood it was very easy to see why people liked him so much. He really was a charmer.

He bustled into the front room and snapped me out of my daydream. 'George, I've got you a little something,' he announced with a grin as large as a Cheshire cat's.

Not used to being gifted anything, I was excited to see what it could be. His hands were behind his back, and therefore I couldn't see what it was. He handed me a contraption, the like of something I'd never seen before. It had a gong on the end of it, and a plate that could be pressed down, to make the gong work. 'What is it?' I asked, trying to sound grateful for the bizarre gift.

'It's a bass drum pedal,' he replied, his grin unfaltering.

'A what?'

'It's to help you play the drums, with your bad leg. You strap this to your leg and all you need to do is press it and it hits the bass drum.'

My face must have fallen open at that point, as he started laughing. It was genuine too. 'You are serious about wanting to learn?'

'Yes,' I gushed.

And that was that.

I had a new passion, a new reason to live. Maybe, finally this would make me popular with the girls, to be honest. I'd tried everything else. When you were not the best looking in school, probably the worst footballer in the whole of Liverpool, and from a broken family that the church didn't want anything to do with, and openly shunned, you needed something to be good at in order to be noticed.

He sat me down at his drum kit and taught me the fundamentals of rhythm. He told me that everything in life had a rhythm, and if I could find that rhythm, the things that made people tick, then I could have everything, and anything, I ever wanted.

It was a lesson I never forgot.

The drums became my whole life, my reason for being. My father was amazed at how quickly I picked it up, telling me I was a natural. He also told me that he thought if I hadn't had a limp, and restricted movement in one of my legs, I could have been one of the greats.

I laughed at this, but I also thought it possible.

I loved George Hogg Senior, more than I'd ever loved my mother. I was glad he'd come back from the war a different man. I don't think I might have loved the man he had been.

Because I never excelled at school, I spent all of my time playing drums, much to the distain of Aunty Joan next door, who would often knock, shouting and balling for me to stop. Whenever my father was home, I noticed she would knock with make-up on, something she never did when I was home alone.

7.

AS THE YEARS rolled by, I began to play in bands. Some of them were talentless hacks who thought playing a trumpet, or strumming a guitar would get them girls. I never stayed with them for long, as I was in this for the long haul. It was going to be a way of life for me, just as it was for my father.

This was my future; I just knew it.

My dad would bring his friends around to play in the lounge, and one particular friend was especially nice to me. He was an old army buddy of his. Tex, they called him. I never did find out why, but this guy could croon. When my father told him about my singing voice, he got me to duet with him, just for laughs. I could tell they were all impressed with what I had to offer, so much so that they took me to a night they were playing in a pub on the Liverpool Dock Road. It was a huge bar, with a stage, and a crowd, and everything you would ever want for a debut singing gig.

It was filled to the rafters with all types. There were sailors, dock workers, people with money, and there were women too.

A lot of women.

My father and Tex called me up on stage to sing along to an old jazz number they were doing. For the life of me I can't even remember what the song was. You'd think something like this would be etched into your brain forever. However, the night was memorable for another reason.

June Carruthers.

When I was on stage, I thought I'd be a nervous wreck. But I wasn't, I took to it like a duck takes to water. All I really remember was an intense feeling of someone watching me. No, it was just watching, it was even staring at me, it was more than that. I know that sounds silly, as I was a sixteen year old boy, signing on a stage with a group of professional musicians, of course I was being watched, but this was so much more… intense. As I sang, I scanned the audience for who it could be. There were so many faces watching, singing along, and talking among themselves.

Then I saw her.

She was young. Maybe a little older than me, but not by much, not like the majority of the other punters. She had red hair that hung down past her shoulders while the rest of it was tied at the back with a ribbon.

She was smiling.

I couldn't tell from on stage, but I guessed she had green eyes, and freckles. She had Irish written all over her.

She was beautiful.

I'd go one step further than that. I would say she was gorgeous.

She sent my timing, and my rhythm into a crazy spiral. I was all over the place. Tex noticed, my father noticed, and the other members of the band noticed too. None of them said anything though, as the punters didn't notice. I learned an important lesson that night, no matter how wrong it goes up there on stage, you just keep on going, as nine times out of ten times, the punters are enjoying themselves far too much to notice.

I composed myself and carried on.

When we were finished, it was to a rapturous applause. It was my first. It was the first of a few firsts that night.

My heart was pounding when I stepped off the stage, and someone shoved a jug of warm, dark ale into my hands. I drank most of it in one gulp as my back was slapped, my hand was shaken, and my hair was ruffled.

I passed through the crowd, searching for the girl with the red hair, everything else was just a blur. I was peripherally aware of Tex mentioning my name from the stage, but it felt like it could have been hundreds of miles away from where my head was.

'I was watching you.'

The voice caught me off guard, as it came from behind. It had a musical, Irish lilt to it. I felt like my heart had missed a beat as I looked to see who the voice belonged to. It turned out I'd been right about the green eyes and the freckles after all. But not about the smile.

It was ten, no, maybe fifteen times better than it had looked from the stage.

'You were watching me?' I asked. I could feel sweat dripping down my neck. I'd never had a girl so beautiful speak to me before, not like this anyway. They'd normally just tease me about my leg, or my height, or one of the thousand other things that were wrong about me, but this one was looking *at* me, smiling *at* me. I felt then how my father must have felt on his return to Bootle. Everyone seemed to love him.

That was how I felt then.

Ten foot tall and bullet proof.

'I was. You have a fantastic voice, for such a young 'un.'

My heart sank then. She was coddling me. I was nothing but a boy to her. I wasn't anything like boyfriend material.

I shrugged, ready to walk away. I'd been hurt too many times before by cruel mouths, I wasn't in the mood to be disappointed now.

'I'm June,' she said, offering me her hand.

'George,' I replied, taking it.

'I know.'

Did I see a blush rising between her freckles? I thought I did. This might have been worth pursuing after all. 'Do you come here often?' I asked, instantly cringing at the stupid question.

She giggled, then shook her head. 'Not really. I was here with my mum, but she's gone for a smoke,' she replied, looking towards the front door of the pub, the one leading out to the dock road.

'Oh, did you not want one?' I asked, more for something to say.

'Do you have any?' Her eyes were flicking around the room as the band continued to play. No one was paying two kids, flirting, any notice.

I grinned and reached into my pocket. 'Half a pack. Do you want one?'

There was a glint in her eye as she nodded. 'I can't let my mum see us though,' she whispered, leaning in close. Her proximity excited me. Her delicate breath on my ear sent tingles right through me. To my embarrassment, I found myself getting too excited, if you know what I mean. This girl was intoxicating. She smelt of soap, cigarette smoke, and a touch of alcohol. It was more inebriating than a fine single malt.

'I know a place,' she whispered. 'Follow me.'

She grabbed my hand. My skin tingled as if electricity was flowing as her fingers interlaced mine, pulling me in the direction she was already moving in. I went willingly, more than willingly. I put my drink down on a table as we passed, almost spilling it in my haste to follow this vision to wherever she wanted me.

I was a willing disciple.

She pulled me through a door I hadn't even noticed before, into a small room that was mostly dark. As she shut it behind us, I remember banging my shin on something, and it hurting really, really badly, as it was my bad leg. However, before I had a chance to voice my pain, her lips were on mine.

Not only her lips, but her tongue was on me too.

As were her hands.

They were all over me.

I can still remember her taste. It was sweet, like she had been drinking wine. There was an aftertaste of cigarettes too. In short, she was delicious.

The smoke was forgotten.

June Caruthers had taken a boy into a small room in the pub and made him a man. I was reborn, right there in the back room of The Griffin.

I'll never forget that night.

It was all over, a little too quick for my liking, but we fell into each other's arms, laughing and giggling.

I was already in love.

That's why what happened next hurt so much.

She fixed herself, and I fixed myself. I didn't know what to say. 'Thank you,' I offered.

She burst out laughing. 'George, you don't have to thank me,' she said. 'I like you. You're cute.'

I had never been called cute before.

'I have to get back out there,' she said.

I was nodding as I leaned over to the door to open it for her. She kissed me on the cheek and left the room, back into the smoky pub. No one noticed us returning, or the ruddy glow and huge grin that was on my face. 'Listen, June. Can I get you a drink?'

She smiled at me and winked.

With my grin still in place I made my way over to the bar and ordered a pint of brown for myself and gin and tonic for her. I breathed in deep. I could still smell her on me, I could taste her on my lips. It was like Heaven. The barman didn't even ask me how old I was, he just gave me the drinks and grinned. 'On the house,' he said. There was a glint in his eye. Did he know what had just happened? Did he know tonight had been the best night of my life?

It turns out he did.

The band had finished their set, and the crowd were applauding. I was nodding, and happy that the night was going so well. I looked around for June, wanting to give her the drink I'd been given for free. I wanted to talk to her, to get lost in her deep green eyes and make plans. I wanted to buy a house, to have children, to grow old together.

Then I saw her.

She was talking to my father.

He was handing her money.

Everything stopped for me right then. My vision tunnelled. Everything else in the bar was a blur. I watched as she accepted the money, it was a couple of notes.

Then she looked right at me.

She smiled.

I'll never forget that smile.

It was sad. It looked desperate, but most of all, what hurt me the most, was the fact that it was filled with pity.

She put the money into her bag, turned, and walked out of the door.

I never saw her ever again.

~~~~

The second memorable thing to happen to me that night came after my heart was broken. At the time it kind of went over my head, and I didn't realise the impact it would have on my life. My heart was broken, my night was ruined, and without even knowing anything about it, my future was about to be changed, forever.

'George, I need to have a word with you,' George Snr spoke, his voice was low, and now that I think about it, it was filled with concern.

I was at least four pints into my cups at this point, not to mention June's gin that I drank myself. The night had been awful, and it was about to get worse.

'Listen son,' he started. As he'd started the sentence with those words, I knew this wasn't going to be a good conversation. 'Me and Tex, well, we've been offered a bit of a run through America.'

He paused for a moment, perhaps waiting for me to say something. I didn't. All I could see was him handing money to June, and her looking at me before walking out of the door.

'Anyway, were leaving tomorrow. We're boarding a ship at the Pier Head. I'll be gone for a year. I'd love it if you came to see me off.'

~~~~

That night I drank more than I had ever drank before, probably more than I've ever drank since. I woke the next morning underneath a bench at the Pier Head. I often wondered if I staggered up there in the hope of seeing my father off on his adventures, or if there were other reasons.

Maybe I was looking for June, walking the streets. Maybe I was looking for other streetwalking girls who serviced the docks. I'll never know. All I knew was I was freezing, I stunk, and was sick to my stomach. With no money in my pockets, I had the long walk back to Bootle to consider, the only warmth; my hands buried deep into my pockets.

8.

I NEVER SAW my father again.

I received a telegram from the USA one fine morning in May, it was from Tex.

> George.
> I regret to inform you that your father, George Hogg Senior, passed away three days ago.
> I will be in touch.
> Tex.

I didn't know what to do with this news. He had been my whole life since my mother ran off with the ex-priest. For the first time in my life, I was truly alone. Yes, he'd been away for a few months, but I always knew he would be coming back, only now, he wasn't. Ever!

It was time to put the anger, and the disappointment behind me, and start to stand on my own two feet. I put my name out into the many music shops around Liverpool, and advertised myself as a singer, and a drummer.

I was offered a lot of auditions as a singer. However, I was never offered one job. I knew why, and it saddened me. No one wanted a stunted cripple fronting their band, no matter how good a singer he was.

The drum jobs however came in hard and fast.

At first the bands were a little taken aback when I would limp into the rehearsal rooms carrying my contraption for my leg. I could hear the excuses brewing in their heads as this strange little man attached himself to the drum kit and awaited instruction on what song to play.

It's fair to say that it gave me smug gratification when after I'd blown them away on the kit, and they offered me the gig, there and then, when I told *them* I'd let them know.

Even with my pronounced limp, I always enjoyed walking out of drum auditions.

~~~~

I found myself a few well-paying gigs and saved up enough money to move into a nice little rental house in Bootle, not far from where I was living in the bed and breakfast I'd moved into after my father's death.

War was brewing in Europe, but it all seemed so far away from Liverpool, and was absolutely nothing to do with me. There was talk of conscription, of activating reserves, of any man within an age range being called up to fight for the cause.

I don't know why, but the idea of fighting in France, or even further afield, excited me, and the male members of the band I was in at the time were all talking about joining up. Everybody knew the first war had dragged on far too long, so it was the consensus that this one would be over by Christmas, after all, this *was* 1939, and not the dark ages.

The real reason I wanted to volunteer was Mary. She was the lead female vocal in the ten-piece band I was in. The male lead was a queen from somewhere down south. He couldn't sing a note and flounced around on stage like the living embodiment of an embarrassment. But the punters loved him, and the chemistry between him and Mary was second to none. They drew the punters in from everywhere. There was even talk of this band going to London to play gigs up that way.

I loved Mary from afar.

I knew who I was, and I knew *what* I was. I also knew someone like her, an angel in human form, was so far out of my reach that I never gave any voice to my feelings.

The club where we played was a dive, out in the suburbs of Liverpool, but luckily for me The Lathom was not far from where I lived. It was run by a nasty type, who's likes I'd seen running a lot of the clubs in Liverpool. He was known simply as Red. He was from London. He was the one trying to find us gigs down that way, as I think he too had a shine for Mary.

I knew she was safe from the likes of him, as a girl like her would never go with someone like him.

I was young, and I was in love. I hadn't been with anyone since June, not the month, the person. The whole experience had left a sour taste in my mouth, and I had never really gotten over it, to be brutally honest with myself. So, when Mary began to show interest in me, I was wary. She was far too beautiful, far too innocent to be attracted to a gargoyle like me.

But she was.

One night after rehearsal, a rehearsal where she'd paid particular interest in me, and my drumming, and where I had been showing off quite a bit, she approached me.

'George, you can really beat those things,' she purred.

I could feel my face and neck redden. I shrugged. 'My dad taught me. He was the one who built this dr…'

'Do you fancy a drink?' she asked, cutting me off mid ramble. I was rather glad she did, as I knew I was about to spill a load of verbal diarrhoea.

'Erm, yes. That would be…'

'Excellent,' she cut me off again, and walked towards the front of the stage. 'Don't run off after rehearsal.'

As she walked away, I noticed the summer dress she was wearing was clinging to every curve she had. The floral pattern, and the yellow fabric enhanced her blonde hair. Even from behind she exuded sensuality, but in an innocent way. My heart was hammering, and I could feel sweat beading around my collar. *Did she really just ask* me *out?* I asked myself, not grasping what had just happened.

There were bigger, and better looking members of the band, and I knew a few of them had expressed their interest in her, and her looks, from drinks after gigs and a bit of boy's talk. I was always amazed that no one had ever taken the step to ask her out on a date.

Maybe it was my turn.

Finally, something was about to go my way.

My timings were out for the rest of the rehearsal. I just couldn't concentrate on what we were playing. Mercifully, after only a few songs, we called it a day, and everyone began to put their instruments away. Mary shot me a few coy glances as everyone began to file out of the hall. I was usually the last to leave, as no one ever thought of helping a cripple with a drum kit.

Today, I didn't mind.

I could see quite a few of the band members offering me sideways glances, as Mary, who was usually first out of the hall, was hanging around, looking for things to do.

After what felt like an eternity, we were alone.

She smiled at me. 'So, where are you taking me?' she asked, her smile was sultry, and to me, she looked every inch the angel I'd always though she was.

I grinned. 'Well, considering I've only had an hour's notice, I was thinking of somewhere like King Dicks in Bootle. It's the only pub I know without sawdust on the floor and no dockers fighting each other.'

She laughed.

That made me feel good.

'Well then, let's go.'

~~~~

We laughed all the way from The Lathom to King Dicks. She was not the person I thought she was. I always had her down as the standoffish type. More interested in her own looks than the needs, or the desires for that matter, of others. But this was not the case. She was very down to earth, and warm. She was funny, and not the slightest bit put out as everyone turned to look at us as we entered the pub.

I knew a few of the regulars, as I only lived a stone throw away, and we drew quite a few looks. They were even more intense as we sat, drank, and laughed, all night.

The looks were even more intense as, after a few hours, we left together. I limped, and swayed a little, with the beautiful Mary on my arm. 'Where are we going now?' she asked as the cool air of the July night hit us both like a steam train.

'Well, I do have a nice bottle of whisky back at my house. My friend Tex had a few shipped over from the USA. He's over there now, touring with his band.'

'Well, that sounds like a plan. Lead on, McDuff!'

I had to laugh. Not everyone would have gotten the Shakespearian quote. This woman was surprising me on every level.

'So, tell me. What's a nice girl like you, doing in a place like this, with a man like me?' I asked as we sat around the small kitchen table, an open bottle of whisky before us, and two glasses poured.

She looked up at me, I could see her eyes were drunk, but the rest of her seemed OK. She shrugged. 'I don't know. Maybe I'm just a sucker for the underdog,' she slurred.

I grinned at her. 'What makes you think I'm the underdog?' I asked, my feelings not even a little bit hurt. I *was* the underdog; I always had been.

'Well, we all know you have a better singing voice than Kevin, and you are the best drummer I've ever worked with. Yet, here you are, in a two-bit swing jazz band, playing in Seaforth, a shitty suburb of Bootle.'

'Well, we all have to start somewhere, don't we? What about you. You're an angel, singing in a two-bit jazz band in Seaforth. Why aren't you working in the bright lights of London? You could make a fortune down there.'

'What makes you think I'm not making a fortune up here?' she asked, taking a sip of her expensive, and exotic whisky.

I shrugged and took a sip from my own glass. 'So, are you?'

'Am I what?'

'Making a fortune.'

She smiled and winked at me. I fell into that wink. Her long blonde hair was flowing, and curling around her shoulders, and her ruby-red lips were leaving intoxicating marks on the glass she was sipping from. I imagined how good it would be to *be* that glass. I looked away; I could feel the flush in my face.

'I get by,' she replied. As she did, she licked the rim of the glass. It was only a small lick, but to me it was the whole world.

'I get by too.' It was my turn to slur my words.

Before long, not long after the not-so-innocent lick of the glass, we were in each other's arms, our lips hungrily reaching for each other, and before I knew anything else, we were rushing up the stairs, we were in the bedroom, and we were naked.

I swear she enjoyed me just as much as I enjoyed her.

~~~~

I fell in love instantly. In truth, I'd been in love with her for months, so when we got together, it was easy to lose myself in her sultry sex appeal. She was as voracious for me as I was for her. When we were not playing, or rehearsing, we were in bed, or drinking, or smoking.

Sometimes it was all three at once.

They were the best three weeks of my life.

Even though it was all a lie, and it was predesigned for me to fall into Red's spiderweb.

She introduced me to gambling. I already had a passing interest in the horses, but she showed me Red's illegal bookmaking enterprise. It was, or so I thought at the time, easy money.

Little did I know the odds were being manipulated in my favour, in order to hook me in. Dreams of all the easy money, and the lavish things I could buy for Mary. I never realised I was being lulled deeper and deeper into the life, when very soon my beginner's luck began to change. My bets were getting larger, and my wins fewer, and further between. The reason I never noticed, was Mary.

She wanted me as much as I wanted her. She could see past my bad leg, my thinning hair, apparently, she loved me for who I was, not what I looked like.

Loved me!

She had said it out loud. She *loved me* for who I was.

I told her I loved her too.

It was then my luck changed again.

Again, for the worse.

'It's a dead cert,' she told me, as we lay in bed, the sheen of sweat was still covering my chest from our exertions, that had culminated minutes before.

'There's no such thing,' I laughed as I lit another cigarette.

She grinned at me, her nakedness, although something I had seen many, many times, was still alluring, and my eyes always gravitated towards it. 'But this one is. Apparently Red knows the owner. I overheard him talking to a shady character the other day. They were talking about two things. Something called The Rialto Ballrooms, and this horse called Prelude. It's a shoo-in to win. They were talking about hobbling the other horses in the race. That means giving them too…'

'Much weight to be able to run,' I finished for her. I was already on the reel.

Hook, line, and sinker.

'Yeah, so they've told the commission that this is the horse's debut on the circuit. They've increased the odds and bet heavy onto it. I think you, or we, should bet on it. I'd go for a month's wages, that way, when it romps home, we can find a little place somewhere, together. We could buy, and then we could live like this forever.'

I was already sold.

As was my soul.

I put the bet on. I couldn't afford it straight off, but Mary had sorted it all out with Red, he told her I could borrow the money from him.

The hook was in.

Red had caught himself a cripple.

9.

MARY BROKE ME.

It was nothing like my mother going away, it was nothing like my father going away, it was nothing like June breaking my heart on that fateful night, this was all to do with my soul, my insides, my heart being pulled from my mouth and stomped on, all over the floor. I wanted nothing more than to crawl into the bottom of the nearest bottle of anything and stay there forever. I wanted to drink the days away and sleep the nights. I didn't want to see anyone.

Only, that wasn't allowed.

I was now deep in Red's pockets, and that was not a good place to be.

It turned out he had a source in London who was bringing in some kind of drug from China, or Japan, or somewhere where it was hot and wet. Red wanted me to distribute these drugs during gigs in the club. He wanted me to get the kids hooked, he called it. To get them wanting, then needing to buy these drugs. And in the meantime, I would be paying off the huge debt I owed.

You see, he wrote in a small clause in my loan, the one I never signed, the one he was now charging me extortionate amounts of interest on.

Basically, if I didn't do this for him, I'd be in debt for years.

In the meantime, Mary disappeared.

She simply never turned up for band practice again.

Ever.

There were no goodbyes, and no notice. There was just no Mary.

I'd sit there, behind my drums, my heart broken, more likely shattered into a million pieces, while people, the few I thought of as friends, asked me over and over where she could be. All I could do was shrug.

Night after night we had to endure Kevin's solo frontman act. It was horrible. All the while I had to mingle with the diminishing punters, trying to offload Red's drugs.

I wondered where she could have gotten to. I wondered if she had ever loved me, or if it had all just been an act. I would fume, I'd smash glasses in my little kitchen after drinking too much whisky from them. I imagined she'd been working with Red all along, and they'd laughed, hysterically, as they deceived me. Then my focus would change, and I'd think that Red had her killed. That she'd worked for him, then fallen for me, and he disposed of her.

I swore that I would, one day, kill Red. It would be my revenge for Mary.

Then everything would change again, and she was in on the deception, a willing partner, fifty-fifty on the downfall of George Hogg.

Bitterness consumed me. It fed from me, consuming everything I held dear. I didn't want to play drums, I didn't want to sing, I didn't want to leave my front door.

But I did.

I had to.

Within one week I had made more money for Red than I owed him. Yet my debt was not even touched. I'd only worked off the interest I owed him. At this rate I realised I would never be able to repay him. I would be in his pockets forever.

The next morning, after a particularly gruelling gig where the Lathom was almost empty, I forced myself to get up extra early. I dressed in my best clothes, and I removed the metal calliper from my bad leg. I walked into Liverpool, the full seven miles, just to stretch my tendons.

I walked into the army recruitment office, and I offered my warrant. I wanted to fight in the war, and to get myself as far from Liverpool, and from Red, as I could.

10.

THE ONLY OPTION available to me was the ARP.

The army couldn't use me. My leg, my *gammy* leg as they so colloquially put it, would not allow me to join the army and see any action abroad. So, I was stuck in Liverpool with my debt to Red, with my memories of Mary, and with my fucking gammy leg.

Thankfully, the war put paid to too many nights out, and Red eventually sold his shares in the Lathom club. He bought a controlling share in The Rialto Ballrooms, up Toxteth way, thankfully, far away from Bootle.

That was the last I saw of him.

For a while anyway.

I gave up the music scene and threw myself into my work with the ARP. We were charged with protecting the home shores. It was out duty to man the air raid sirens, and make sure the windows were blacked out in the case of an enemy air raid.

Living in Bootle, so close to the main docks, and the port of Liverpool, we were in imminent danger of attack, and it was our job to patrol the area, making sure the lights were out, and the heavy blackout curtains were drawn. If they weren't, we were to write the address down and hand it over to the authorities. Heavy fines were levied for anyone caught breaking these rules, and with Bootle not exactly being an affluent area, very few people did flaunt them.

Occasionally there would be some excitement, but mostly the night patrols were humdrum, boring walks around cold, wet streets. With my long black coat on, and my black tin hat with ARP plastered over the front, like a vampire I stalked the streets of Bootle searching for offenders.

11.

IT WAS A cold, wet, and dark Friday night. My leg had been killing me all day, and I was in no mood for a patrol. However, there had been intelligence, talk of an air attack on the docks. It had been assumed, with Hitler's close connections to Liverpool, they had been marked as a strategic target for the Luftwaffe, a good way to destroy the supply chains of the UK.

Even with all the excited chatter, I still couldn't be bothered tonight. I'd drunk far too much last night, drowning my sorrows about Mary, and had been suffering all day. I'd been so bad that I was considering contracting Red for some of his *snow*. I knew a little bit of that would take the edge off this stinking hangover.

I didn't though.

I didn't need that level of negativity, not to mention inconvenience, in my life.

I was *still* reeling from Mary. Even though it had been months since she'd disappeared, she was still there. She was in every dream; she was there every time I closed my eyes. Every time I heard a female voice, I expected to see her when I turned. I expected to see her, dressed in the damned yellow sundress, her long blonde hair falling down over her shoulders.

Every time I was disappointed.

I was more than disappointed.

I was heartbroken.

Still.

As I pulled my collars up around my ears to stave off the cold, I grabbed my torch, my gas mask, and made my way out of the little house.

Bootle was dark, and it was quiet.

Just once around the park, I thought as I tightened the straps of my tin hat around my chin. *Then back home, feet up and* no *whisky tonight.*

I was looking forward to an uneventful evening patrol, and an early night as I stepped out into the cold.

~~~~

I hated Derby Park at the best of times, but especially at night. It wasn't spooky, or anything like that, it was just that there were a lot of places where people could hide to escape the curfew enforced for public safety. Keeping an eye on the sky, and an ear out for the rumble of aeroplane engines, I headed into the darkness of the green space. *After all, it's my duty to the King and country.*

I heard them straight away.

Giggling.

My stomach dropped as I now knew I had work to do. *Fucking kids,* I thought as I dragged my leg, that had been playing up due to the cold and wet weather, into the park.

'Is anyone there?' The moment the shout left my lips, the giggling stopped.

'I said, is there anyone there? I'm an ARP warden. You need to get out of this park and get yourselves into a shelter. There's intelligence there'll be a raid at some point tonight.'

They were on the bandstand.

There were two of them.

They were young, and they were drunk. Two girls, one blonde, and the other dark.

I rolled my eyes, letting out a sigh. This was going to be a pain in the backside, but it *was* my duty to keep them safe.

'Come on you two, get up and get home. It's not safe in the blackout,' I snapped testily at them. 'Where do your parents think you are, anyway?' I asked, despairing in the way some people brought their children up these days.

'Won't we be OK now that there's a big, strong ARP warden here to look after us?' one of the girls quipped.

I swung the torch around and illuminated both their faces. I would have guessed they were sixteen, maybe a little older, or even younger, you can never tell these days. They were both very good looking girls either way. The blonde was a real beauty, but she paled into insignificance next to the dark haired one.

She was strikingly beautiful.

My brain mixed them up.

It put the blonde hair on the dark haired girl, and it come up with Mary. My eyes began to sting. I was tearing up. *Why had she left me? Why do all women leave me? Am I so abhorrent that my mother had to go, June had to leave, and then Mary.*

'Come on, I'm going to have to get you home, or at least somewhere safe until you sober up.' My heart wasn't in it. All I wanted to do was to get home and crawl back into that bottle I'd opened, but never finished, last night. *There goes my early night,* I thought without a hint of irony.

'Oh, look, Mary. He can't keep his hands to himself,' the blonde girl laughed as I reached out and grabbed her friend.

My eyes widened at the mention of the name. I turned to look at her. My brain had gotten it all wrong. *She was Mary.*

I was confused now.

As I looked at them, my brain was swapping faces at an alarming rate. It made me sick to my stomach as I watched their faces merge, come apart, and then merge again. I couldn't tell which way was up, and which way was down.

'Shut your mouth, you *slut,*' I spat.

After that, I have no idea what happened.

That night truly is a blur to me.

All I remember is a frenzy of movement. I remember the dark haired girl shuffling away, threatening me with her family, her brothers. I had no idea where the other one had gone. Her face was etched into my brain though. I can still see her to this day. How had she gotten away, leaving me with this… this *slut*, I'll never know.

I hated that word.

But in my rage, my confusion about what was happening, it was the only word I could use to describe how I felt towards this girl. She *was* a slut, and she *had* led me on, and there was no way I was going to allow her to tell her brothers what had happened tonight.

There was a lose piece of masonry on the bandstand. I reached for it, as the girl continued to curse, and shout, and threaten.

I could feel it in my hands. It was dry. It had been under the cover of the bandstand. My hands felt musty, dirty, as my fingers wrapped around it.

I enjoyed the weight of it.

'You don't know who my family are, do you? My dad and uncles are going to hunt you down. You're not going to be hard to find when I tell them a troll, with a gammy leg attacked me. When they find you, they'll rip your…'

She had her back to me, and never knew anything about it, as I hit her with the brick.

I just swung it, without even thinking. The connection to her head felt strange. It shut her up, instantly. That part was good, but as it connected, the thud, and reverberation up my arm, was sickening. She fell onto the wooden boards of the bandstand, face first. I dropped my weapon and flipped her over. I have no idea what came over me, but suddenly this girl was my mother, then she was June, then she was Mary. Then finally, she was the dark haired girl on the bandstand.

I wrapped my hands around her neck, and I squeezed.

I didn't know if she was already dead at that point, or if I was killing her, but I didn't care.

Her eyes opened, and I watched them roll within their sockets. Her mouth twitched, it opened as she tried to speak, maybe to shout for help.

I continued to squeeze. She was fighting me, and then suddenly… she wasn't.

At that moment the world went crazy. I though the devil himself had come to take me below for taking the innocence, and then the life, of this young lady. The noise was deafening, and the blast was hot and horrendous.

When it passed, when the madness of the bombing raid was over and I could survey the scene, an idea came to me. It was hideous, and it was gruesome, but it was one that might just save me from swinging in the gallows. I knew how to get rid of the body.

Mary, I was sure that wasn't her name, was about to become a casualty of war.

12.

I GOT AWAY with the murder. It wasn't my finest moment. I felt for the family. Apparently, they were a large Italian family who ran some bakeries in the city. Everyone knew they were a front for their real businesses, illegal gentlemen's clubs in the centre of Liverpool.

I kept my head low for the rest of the war. I helped in the clean-up of Bootle, and I thought about attending the girl's funeral. I even fantasised about getting a thank you from her father for trying to save her life.

Again, it wasn't my finest hour.

I vowed then I was going to clean up my act, just like the clean-up of Bootle. I was going to go back to doing what I loved best. I had a friend, well, when I say friend, he was an acquaintance more than anything else. He was a strange type, I was almost sure he was a queen, but he kept himself to himself, and I didn't mind that. He played the trombone, and a number of other wood and brass instruments in a swing band in The Rialto Ballrooms.

It was a club whose name I'd heard before, but for the life of me I couldn't remember where from.

I went along, did my audition as the dutiful drummer, and was pleasantly surprised to see that it was father's old friend, Tex, who was the lead male vocal.

He vouched for me, and I got the job.

I was now the drummer in The Downswing Seven, the resident band in The Rialto. They seemed a very pleasant bunch of people to work with, and the female lead was a knockout. She could sing, and she had the looks. I thought she might be someone to help me forget about Mary.

So, my first live gig is tomorrow night, and I couldn't be more excited. Apparently, the owner of the club wants to have a meeting with us all after the gig, just to let us know the lay of the land.

He's from down south.

His name is Red.

This is going to be interesting!

A Prelude to Murder

AUTHOR'S NOTES

I LOVE GEORGE Hogg, I think I will always have a soft spot for this fella. I don't think he's the nasty person we have grown to love to hate. I think he is a victim of his own circumstances.

This short story came to me in a flash, and I wanted to write it as a special for the Kickstarter campaign for SING SING SING FOR MURDER.

A few people took up the option on the book, and I have never known if they have ever read it, or if they did, enjoyed it.

I'm putting this out now as a little prequel for George, before I embark on the very las novel in the ...FOR MURDER series, this will be called SWINGING FOR MURDER, and *should* wrap up all the loose ends in the series. I say *should* because it's not written yet (just fleshed out), and you just never know what's going to happen.

I love a bit of nostalgia, and I thought George would love to travel down a bit of memory lane, so this is the story about how a talented, but sad little boy grew up to be the man we find in IN THE MOOD FOR MURDER, and SING SING SING FOR MURDER.

~~~~

Big thank yous go out to Lisa Lee Tone for all the help she had given me in my entire writing career.

Lauren Davies has had to live with me, and my array of the other characters who live in my head, every single day of the week.

The girls Grace and Sian for pretty much having to be dragged through my ambition to do something with my writing for all these years.

Kelly Rickard for all the proof reading she does for me. Honestly, she hasn't let me down yet.

Wyndham Price for his unending devotion to a piece of work he never had any stake in, but just totally believed in the project. At the time of writing these notes, we have our fingers, toes, eyes, legs, and anything else we can cross for some exciting news.

And of course, Tony Bolland. Without Tony's devotion to detail and his ability to research and offer some of the maddest (true) stories about the Merseyside music scene, this series would have been dead in the water a long time ago.

But most of all… A huge thank you to YOU, the readers. The ones who have stuck with me on this journey into the fiery depths of Hell, and back again. Please stick with me, and there will be more to come.

THANK YOU, THANK YOU, THANK YOU…

Dave McCluskey
Liverpool
June 2024

www.ingramcontent.com/pod-product-compliance
Lightning Source LLC
Chambersburg PA
CBHW070811120626
46557CB00002B/816